A fiSH out of water

by Wesley Eure
co-creator of the *Dragon Tales*

Designed and Illustrated
by Meredith College Art Department

PELICAN PUBLISHING COMPANY
Gretna 2000

Printed in Hong Kong
Published by Pelican Publishing Company, Inc.
1000 Burmaster Street, Gretna, Louisiana 70053

This book is dedicated to all who face the impossible.

A UNIQUE COLLABORATION

Born out of a unique idea from Brooks Britt, *A Fish Out of Water* was illustrated and designed by art students at Meredith College in Raleigh, North Carolina. Founded in 1891, Meredith is the Southeastern United States' largest private women's college with a long history of shaping talented artists. *A Fish Out of Water* was illustrated by the Advanced Illustration class under the direction of Linda FitzSimons, Associate Professor of Art. The book design and, in particular, the innovative typography were undertaken by the Advanced Graphic Design class under the direction of Regina Schindler Rowland, Assistant Professor of Art.

The illustrations were created with cut-paper collage and handmade textures. The composition of each illustration from the viewpoints of the bird and fish characters was accomplished with simple, bold, colorful shapes that would create strong, eye-catching designs. The text on each page was designed to flow with the action and movement of the story and to compliment not merely describe the illustrations in a unique, interpretive manner. The collaboration between the two classes extended to a unique fusion of illustration, book design, and typography, each area contributing equally to the success of the entire project.

Illustrators: Shelley Brown, Ching-Hui Chen, Karen Haisty, Susan Jones, Gail Lambert, Allison Lane, Corie Long, Amy Patterson, Rebecca Renn, Emily Stephens, Anna Taylor, and Tracy Vincent

Graphic Designers: Erika Baker, Kari Becker, Madge Duffy, Christie Evans, Brigitte Ting, and Martha Walton

Art Directors: Linda FitzSimons and Regina Schindler Rowland

Special Thanks to Christie Evans, Rebecca Renn, and Brigitte Ting for their extraordinary efforts in the final stages of this project, as well as to Wesley Eure, who contributed suggestions to the students' ideas, and of course to Brooks Britt, who initiated this collaboration.

It was unbelievable. All the **animals** agreed it would not work.

They were from **two** **2** diff**e**r**e**nt worlds.

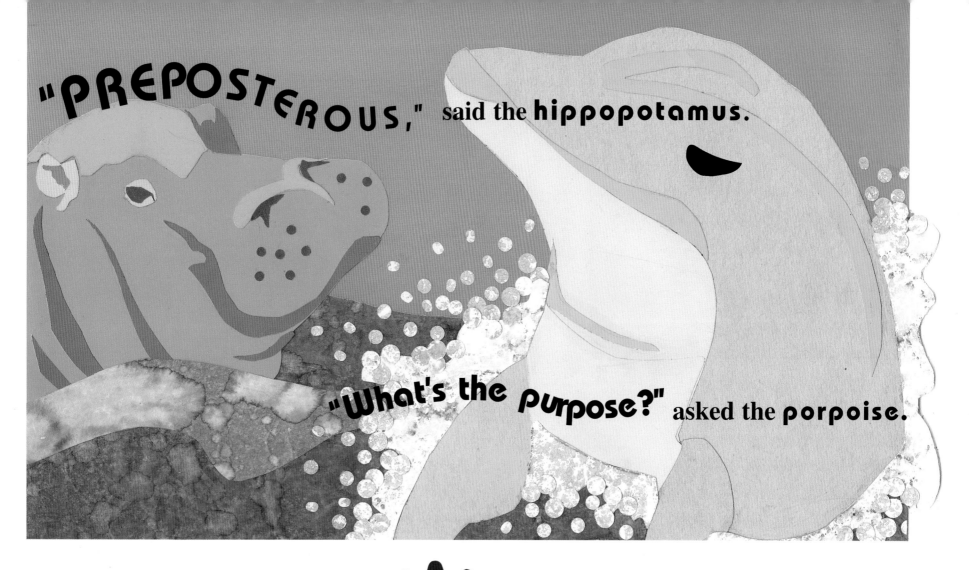

"PREPOSTEROUS," said the hippopotamus.

"What's the purpose?" asked the porpoise.

But it was true. A bird & a fish had fallen in love.

It started simply.

On a cliff high above the ocean, the 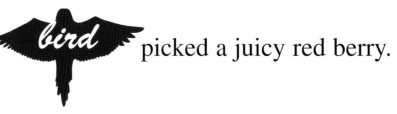 picked a juicy red berry.

Suddenly, it slipped out of her beak.

The berry *splashed* into the water

and almost hit the *fish*.

"what luck!" gurgled the  fish

as it ate the **big** red berry.

The  *bird* swooped down and cried,

"That was mine!"

The *fish* poked its head out of the water and said,

"sorry, i thought it fell from a tree."

The 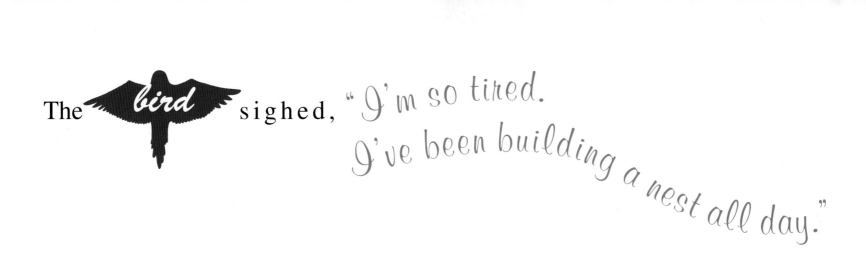 sighed, "I'm so tired. I've been building a nest all day."

"wait Here and i'LL repay you," promised the fish.

The  dove to the bottom of the o c e a n and returned
with a large piece of seaweed.

"this is for your nest," smiled the .

The  bird was overjoyed!

"Now I will have a place to sleep tonight," sang the bird and flew away with the seaweed.

Day after day the  **bird** & the **fiSH** met.

The **bird** brought gifts of rare berries.

And the **fiSH** brought gifts of seaweed and pearls.

The  taught the *fish* to s i n g .

And the *fish* taught the  *bird* g r e a t s e c r e t s of the sea.

Soon, the  bird & the fish fell in love.

The 's family scolded,

"He's not your kind. Some fish eat birds.

Besides, a bird can't live under water!"

The fish's family scolded,

"She's not your kind. Some birds eat fish.

Besides, a fish can't live out of water."

The *bird* and the *fiSH* were *ɕad*.

They wanted their families to be *happy* for them.

"Why does my family only see how different we are?" cried the bird.

"WHY CAN'T MY FAMILY SEE HOW aLike we are?" cried the fish.

"i wiſH i could breathe out of water," sighed the **fiſH**.

"I wish I could breathe under water," sighed the **bird**.

A **mermaid** secretly listening
said she could magically grant their wishes.

The  the fish were so happy.

"i will live with you in your nest," smiled the 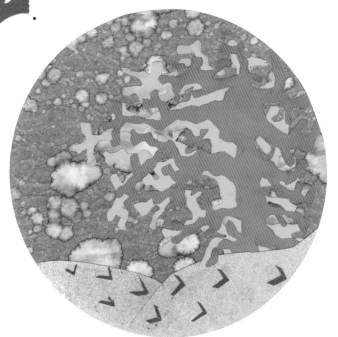 fish.

"I will live with you in your coral reef," smiled the bird.

But the mermaid warned,

"One of you must give up everything you have known to live in the other's world."

The **bird** thought about never again *flying* high above the trees.

The **fish** thought about never again *swimming* in the **cool** ocean.

And both the **bird** & the **fish** knew they would miss their families.

"thank you for your offer," said the  to the mermaid.

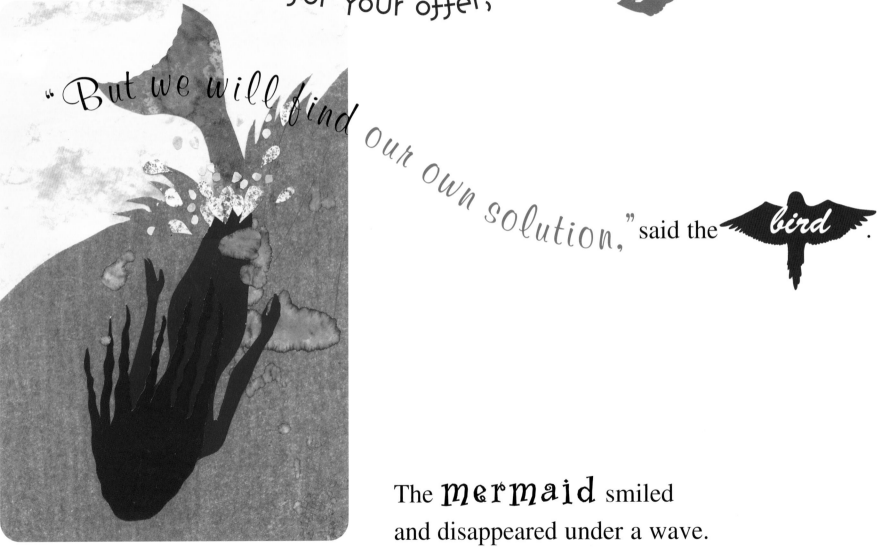

"But we will find our own solution," said the bird.

The **mermaid** smiled
and disappeared under a wave.

The  knew what they had to do.

The 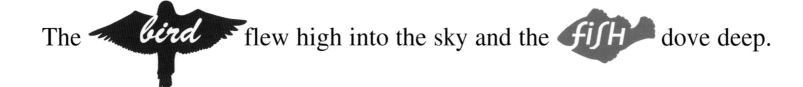 flew high into the sky and the fish dove deep.

Many weeks later, hundreds of **animals** gathered on shore,
while thousands of birds circled over head.

Suddenly, a SEAGULL shouted,

"HERE THEY COME!"

What a sight it was!

The  sprang from under the water.

They sailed on the air for a time
and then dove into the sea.

A minute later they flew into the air once more.

All the animals **cheered!**

Even the *fiSH* 's and the *bird* 's families cheered.

You see, the 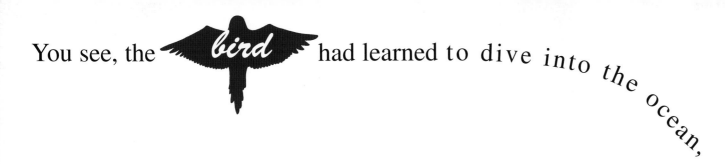 **bird** had learned to dive into the ocean,

while the **fish** had learned to leap out of the sea.

For many hours each day, the **bird** & the **fish** **laughed** and **played**.

The 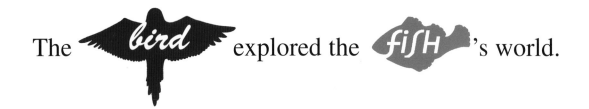 explored the fish's world.

And the fish shared the 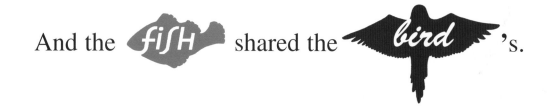's.

They had each learned to live in the other's world.

The  End